W9-AVC-473

# In Trouble with Teacher

# In Trouble with Teacher

PATRICIA BRENNAN DEMUTH

ILLUSTRATED BY TRUE KELLEY

DUTTON CHILDREN'S BOOKS

NEW YORK

**MAY 9 6**

*J*

*Library of Congress Cataloging-in-Publication Data*

Demuth, Patricia.
In trouble with teacher / by Patricia Brennan Demuth;
illustrated by True Kelley.—1st ed.
p.    cm.
Summary: Third grader Montgomery draws great pictures
and writes wonderful stories, but he's afraid that his teacher
only cares about his terrible spelling.
ISBN 0-525-45286-9
[1. Teacher-student relationships—Fiction.
2. English language—Spelling—Fiction. 3. Schools—Fiction.
4. Self-perception—Fiction.]    I. Kelley, True, ill.    II. Title.
PZ7.D4122In  1995  [Fic]—dc20  94-33183  CIP  AC

Published in the United States by
Dutton Children's Books,
a division of Penguin Books USA Inc.
375 Hudson Street, New York, New York 10014
Designed by Carolyn Boschi
Printed in U.S.A.
First Edition
1  3  5  7  9  10  8  6  4  2

*For my beautiful nieces—*
*Brandy and Stacey Else*
P.B.D.

*To the teachers at the*
*Simonds School*
T.K.

# One

**M**ontgomery woke up knowing he was in trouble. The trouble lay low in the back of his mind. Montgomery tried to hide from it. He pulled the pillow over his head. But the trouble marched to the front anyway.

The trouble was with the teacher, Mrs.

Wix. Montgomery didn't know his spelling words. Today was the test.

Montgomery was sure to flunk.

The teacher was sure to scold.

Montgomery hugged his pillow tightly. Mom came in and rolled up the shade.

"Rise and shine," she said cheerfully.

"Bumph noof oopmfa ufn fhul," said Montgomery from under the pillow.

"Come again?" said Mom.

Montgomery stuck his head out.

"I'm not going to school," he said. "I'm sick."

Mom said, "Hmmm, let's take a look."

She came to the bed and placed her hand on Montgomery's forehead. "No fever."

She gazed deeply into his eyes.

Montgomery put on his sickest look.

"You *look* fine," said Mom.

Montgomery groaned and pulled the pillow back over his head. When Mom left, he thought about ways to be sick. He wished he could throw up or something. Maybe if he poured oatmeal into the toilet . . .

No. Mom would never believe it. She'd say, "Hmmm, let's take a look."

And that would be the end of that.

# Two

**M**ontgomery put on a clean T-shirt and went to brush his teeth. He frowned at himself in the mirror. Bad move. The frown reminded him of how Mrs. Wix looked when she got mad. It was not a pretty sight.

Deep ruts dug into her brow.

Her green eyes turned to ice.

Her long finger pointed and wagged.

So far, Montgomery had not been scolded by Mrs. Wix. This was the fourth week of third grade—and so far no frowns had fallen upon him. Montgomery sat in the very last row in the very back of the room. It was quiet back there—just like Montgomery was.

He had watched Mrs. Wix get mad at *others*, though. Especially Ju-Ju Bee. Montgomery wouldn't want to be Ju-Ju Bee for anything.

Last week, Ju-Ju Bee got scolded for chew-

ing gum. When Mrs. Wix walked by, he tried to hide the gum in his ear. The gum was purple. Mrs. Wix saw it.

She made him take the gum out of his ear and go to the front of the class. He had to hold it in his hand while she scolded. The ball of gum looked wet and sticky.

Montgomery watched the scolding. He felt safe and far away. He also felt a little bad for Ju-Ju Bee.

But today . . . Today the action wouldn't be so far away.

Today was Friday. Every Friday there was a spelling test. Every spelling test had twenty words. Every word was worth five points. If you missed more than six words, you flunked.

If you flunked, Mrs. Wix didn't hand you your paper right away. You had to march to the front of the class to get it back. All the kids watched.

Montgomery had never been part of the Flunkers' March. Three Fridays had passed since school started. Three spelling tests. And Montgomery had passed each one (with two close calls).

Montgomery pulled off his pajama top. He shivered. He could feel ice from a pair of green eyes.

# Three

**M**ontgomery sat watching his cornflakes turn soggy.

"Montgomery, what's wrong?" asked his mother.

Montgomery thought about telling her the truth: "I'm going to flunk my spelling test."

Then Mom would say: "Why?"

And he would tell his mom: "Because I don't know the words. But it's not my fault. See, Monday I got the list of words. And I did look at them. I looked at them long enough to see they were real hard. I made up my mind right then: I would study on Tuesday.

"But that was impossible. *The Return of the Green Ape* was on TV, and our VCR is broken, as you know, so I couldn't tape it, and of course I couldn't *miss* it.

"So on Wednesday I did look at the spelling words again. I remember remembering that the words were extra hard. But I still had a day left. I figured I'd do best to save up my energy. Then I'd give it my all on the last day.

"So Thursday—last night—I couldn't wait to study. First I did my other homework. Just when I got to spelling, Katy ran in. She said I took her skateboard, which I didn't, and we ran downstairs to tell you, Mom. And then I noticed Teddy was finishing off my game of Nintendo. And then Katy found her skateboard under the couch. By then, I was showing Teddy how to capture the flag without dying. It took a while because Ben called in the middle. And then, just when I was about to study spelling, you said it was bedtime.

And so how can I help but flunk when you made me go to bed, Mom?"

Suddenly, Montgomery's thoughts were interrupted. Mom said, "This is Earth, calling Mars. What's wrong?"

Montgomery sighed. "Nothing," he said. He didn't want his mom to feel bad about making him flunk the spelling test.

# Four

**A**s usual, Ben saved a seat on the bus for Montgomery. Ben was Montgomery's best friend. Today he had a cold.

Montgomery sat down and pulled out his list of spelling words. The words were still there, all right—all twenty of them, frowning up at him.

Ben's nose was running. He didn't have a tissue. *Sniffle, sniffle,* he went.

"Hey, Ben," said Montgomery, "you could be a track star if you ran as fast as your nose."

"Good one!" said Ben. He looked through his backpack to find a big red notebook. Inside the notebook were Ben and Montgomery's best jokes. The boys planned to work together when they grew up. They were going to write a comic strip. The notebook already had 351 jokes to get them started.

Montgomery looked back at his spelling list. He sighed. Spelling was his worst subject. There were so many spelling rules to learn, so many exceptions to every rule.

One day the class was studying long *e*. Mrs. Wix wrote a hint on the board:

These six words were the six different spellings for long *e*, she explained. Montgomery felt excited. He was sure he could memorize those six words. Then he would know the spellings of long *e* forever.

Then Montgomery realized the bad news. There were thousands of words with long *e*'s. You had to memorize which ones had which spellings. And then you had to remember how to spell the *other* sounds in those words. And then, you had to learn other rules for short *e*. Not to mention spelling rules for other long vowels—like *a* and *i* and *u*. And so on and so on—on to spelling eternity, where angels wore a long *o* above their heads.

Montgomery sighed—a short *u* sound. He looked back at his spelling list. The first words were *knee, knit, knock*. Montgomery glanced down the list to the longest word: *elephant*. "E-L-E-P-H-A-N-T," said Montgomery to himself. "What kind of way is *that* to spell elephant?" The people who invented spelling didn't know how to spell! Any kid could tell them that *elephant* has an *f* in the middle, not a *p*!

Montgomery himself could tell them how to spell elephant: *alifunt!*

"Elephant!" muttered Montgomery aloud.

Ben frowned. He was big for his age.

"Not you," said Montgomery. "It's a spelling word."

Ben relaxed. "Elephant's easy," he said. "E-L-E-P-H-A-N-T! I can spell hippopotamus, too. Bet you can't spell that."

"Bet I can. T-H-A-T."

Ben reached for the notebook again. Montgomery was glad that Ben was a good speller. Ben was going to *write* their comic strip. Montgomery would *draw* it.

Maybe today he could draw a picture of an elephant for the spelling test. Curved ivory tusks. Long nose like a hose.

No. Mrs. Wix would frown and ask for a caption. One that was spelled correctly.

# Five

During science class, Mrs. Wix talked about animals that migrate. What a great idea, thought Montgomery. How pleasant to migrate—like right now, to the South Pole or somewhere else.

Mrs. Wix was wearing her charm bracelet.

Every time she moved, the silver charms jangled. They jangled Montgomery's nerves.

Beatrice sat across from Montgomery. She was waiting for the teacher to ask a question so she could give the right answer. Montgomery knew that she would know all the right answers for the spelling test, too. Beatrice always got 110 percent on her spelling tests. The extra ten points were for the extra-credit words.

Thoughts of the spelling test pinched at Montgomery's stomach. He pictured himself writing down all the wrong spellings. It was terrible knowing that all the right answers would be just *inches* away—on Beatrice's paper. It was like dying of thirst in the desert while your neighbor had a six-pack of soda!

Montgomery stared at Beatrice's long

braids. Under those braids was a brain. Inside that brain were all the right spelling words. At this very moment, those words were floating around her brain. When Beatrice called, the words would swim to the front.

Montgomery had heard about mind reading. Maybe if he stared long enough, he could see into Beatrice's mind. He could read all the spelling words in there—even *elephant*.

Just then, Beatrice turned around and stared at Montgomery! So did the other kids! Mrs. Wix, too!

"Montgomery," said the teacher. "I'm sure you can name an animal."

"Uh . . . elephant?" Montgomery guessed.

The kids giggled. Beatrice laughed out loud. Then she swung around and waggled her hand in the air. "I can, I can!"

"Yes, Beatrice?" said Mrs. Wix.

"Birds! Birds fly south in winter!"

Ben held up a note to Montgomery. It said, "Bad one."

It wasn't supposed to be a joke, thought Montgomery.

He slumped in his chair. He wished there *were* flying elephants who would carry him south on their large gray backs. He would sit right in the middle of the elephant—right where the *f* belongs.

# Six

**G**ood thing art class was on Friday. Montgomery looked forward to seeing what the art teacher was wearing. She always wore something she made herself. All her jewelry was homemade—from things like wood, wire, stones, or buttons. Once she had even carved animals out of meat bones. She put the animals on a chain made out of bottle caps. When she wore that necklace, it looked like a safari marching around her neck.

Today she wore a T-shirt she had painted herself. On the front was the head of a big cow. On the back was the rear end of the cow, its tail swishing flies.

"Yea!" said the class when they found out they were going to paint their own T-shirts, too.

The art teacher explained that first they would all pick out animals to draw on their shirts. (It didn't take Montgomery long to think of one.) "Today you'll draw the animals on paper," she said. "Next week, you can paint them on the T-shirts."

Handing out sketch paper, she said, "Remember, imagination counts."

"I do, too," said Montgomery. "One, two, three, four."

The art teacher laughed. She smiled at Montgomery as if he was sunshine after the rain.

Montgomery went to work drawing a flying elephant. He thought how lovely smiles from teachers were. Beside him, Ben was drawing an elephant, too. Ben couldn't draw very well. To make him feel better, Montgomery said, "Nice elephant. Neat trunk."

"It's a parrot," said Ben. "That's the beak."

For a moment both boys looked glum. Then they burst out laughing.

Ben looked over at Montgomery's elephant picture. "Nice parrot," he joked.

Montgomery went back to work. He made the ears extra huge—huge enough to be wings that could carry him through the clouds.

Then he started to think about the smiling teacher he had had for both first and second grades, Miss Pink. She used to sit right down on the floor during reading circle. Reading was almost as hard as spelling for Montgomery. But Miss Pink was really nice about it. She knew Montgomery was embarrassed to read out loud. So she skipped him. For almost two years, Montgomery never had to take his turn in reading circle.

*Then* came third grade. *Then* came Mrs. Wix.

The first time Mrs. Wix called on him to read out loud, Montgomery said, "I'll pass."

"Pardon me?" Mrs. Wix frowned.

"Can I pass?" he said.

"This is not a card game, Montgomery. Please read!"

So Montgomery read. His part was about a guy waiting at the train station. Montgomery mispronounced *depot*. He said, "The poor boy waited long at the dee-pot." Everyone laughed. Montgomery blushed.

Later Ben gave him this cartoon:

Montqomery + de pot

"So funny that I forgot to laugh," said Montgomery.

He was sure Mrs. Wix would regret her

mistake. But next time, she called on him to read *again*. And she hadn't stopped, either. She acted as though Montgomery could read like anybody else.

The art teacher was walking around the class, looking at everyone's picture. "Oh, Montgomery!" she said over his shoulder. "Marvelous elephant! I just *love* those purple ears!"

She moved on to Ben. "How clever of you to draw an aardvark, Ben," she said.

"It's a parrot," Ben groaned.

Montgomery and Ben stared glumly at Ben's picture. Then they burst into another set of giggles.

# Seven

**M**ontgomery decided to study spelling during social studies. He put the word list on his lap. But he was afraid he would look weird always glancing down. Maybe people would think he had wet his pants or something.

So Montgomery put the list inside his

math book and propped the book open on his desk. The words started to swim in front of him. He kept reading the list over and over. Not learning it, just reading.

Montgomery was thinking about the Flunkers' March again. Mrs. Wix didn't call it that, but Montgomery did. Mrs. Wix always said something to the flunkers after they marched up to the front. Montgomery couldn't hear exactly what she said. But he could guess.

"You lousy rotten speller, you!" she probably said.

"Can you spell 'flunk'?"

"I can't believe what I am seeing. Is your
brain in your big toe?"

Last week Montgomery had seen Mrs. Wix reach into her desk for something. "Don't shoot," he wanted to say. She handed something to the flunker. Probably a rock—standing for rock head. Or maybe a list of extra homework: look up one thousand words in the dictionary.

Today Montgomery imagined what he might say back to the teacher when he took his turn up there. Mrs. Wix would say, "You ought to be ashamed of yourself."

"Oh, I am," Montgomery would say. He would bow his head to prove it.

"Well, you should be more ashamed."

"I am!" He would bend over further.

"Even more."

And he would keep stooping—down,

down. By the time he walked back to his desk, he would be on his knees, ashamed as could be. All the kids in their seats would look down at him as if he were a bug.

Montgomery felt a poke. It was Beatrice's finger. "Wake up!" she said. Beatrice was handing him his spelling list. It had fallen down, down—to the floor.

"These words are easy," she whispered.

"Yeah, right," Montgomery mumbled. "Thanks."

# Eight

**A**t recess, the guys chose baseball captains. The captains started picking their teams. "Montgomery!" called out the first captain.

Montgomery was usually one of the first two guys picked. Ju-Ju Bee was the other.

"Can't play today," said Montgomery. "Got to study."

"Then Ju-Ju Bee!" called out the captain.

Montgomery sat down near the field. He pulled the list of spelling words out of his back pocket. He counted up the easy words. Only five. That left fifteen he didn't know. He could miss five and still pass. So he'd have to learn ten new words. Montgomery counted up again. Maybe he knew six words. Let's see, what score would he get then.

"Two to three," someone shouted. It was the baseball score. Two to three already, Montgomery thought. Ju-Ju Bee's team was losing. What an exciting game. Montgomery started watching out of the corner of his eye.

Ju-Ju Bee's team was up to bat. Montgomery hoped the *other* team would win. He

was used to playing against Ju-Ju Bee. They were always on different teams because they were always the first two guys picked.

In the bottom of the third inning, Ben was the first batter up. He made a base hit. "Solid hit up the middle," Montgomery said to himself. While Ben ran to first base, Montgomery stole a glance at his spelling list.

Ju-Ju Bee was the next batter. Montgomery jumped up and waved his spelling paper at the guys in the outfield. "Move back!" he called. "Get ready for Ju-Ju Bee."

Ju-Ju Bee was a home-run hitter. He could send that ball sailing. And when he did, Montgomery was always ready . . . that is, when he was playing.

Usually Montgomery played left field. He loved every part of it:

running to meet the ball;

grabbing it out of the air;

hearing the solid smack as the ball hit his
leather glove;

hurling the ball to the infield or home.

Roger was playing left field now. Lucky for Ju-Ju Bee.

At home plate, Ju-Ju Bee pawed at the ground like a horse. That was his good-luck move.

The first two pitches were foul tips. But on the third, Ju-Ju Bee let loose. *Whomp!*

Montgomery began to jump up and down at the crack of the bat. He longed to chase that ball. It was flying far and left.

Roger saw the ball coming. He lifted his glove to the heavens—as if he was praying, Montgomery thought.

God wasn't listening. The ball bounced off Roger's glove.

Ben ran home. The score was tied: 3–3.

Ju-Ju Bee rounded second base. He passed third. Roger was looking around for the ball. When he found it, he threw it to home plate. Kicking up a cloud of dust, Ju-Ju Bee came sliding in.

"Out!" yelled the catcher as he reached down to tag Ju-Ju Bee.

"I'm safe!" yelled Ju-Ju Bee.

The two teams started yelling at each other:

*Out!*

*Safe!*

*Out!*

"Safe!" yelled Montgomery. "I saw it!"

Ju-Ju Bee turned surprised eyes on Montgomery. So did the others. But nobody argued. Ju-Ju Bee's team won: 4–3.

The bell rang. Montgomery picked up his dusty spelling paper. When he ran on line, Mrs. Wix was hurrying everyone along.

Montgomery held his spelling paper up to his face. He hoped Mrs. Wix would see how hard he was studying.

"Montgomery, don't dawdle. Catch up in line there" was all she said.

# Nine

**M**ontgomery noticed the big poster as soon as he walked back into the room. It said:

Mrs. Wix changed the poster every week. Last week it had said:

SPELLING COUNTS!

IT'S THE DIFFERENCE BETWEEN

A

DESERT and DESSERT.

And the week before that, it was:

Miss Pink had acted as if spelling didn't matter that much. She used to have the class write lots of stories, and she would never point out the misspelled words. She had pasted colorful stickers on top of all of Montgomery's stories. They said things like "Super!" and "Writing Star."

Montgomery's mom hung all his stories on the refrigerator door. Every time Montgomery got a glass of milk, he would stand and reread both the stories and the stickers.

Last week Mrs. Wix had asked the class to write a story. Montgomery wrote about a shy whale who was too big to hide. The whale would hold his breath so that he didn't have to go to the top of the water. Then by the time he couldn't hold it any longer and had to swim to the top, he'd let out such a

big gush of air that it caused a cyclone and he attracted more attention than ever.

As usual, Montgomery really got into writing the story. By the time he'd finished, he was nearly popping. He'd been holding his breath, too!

When Montgomery got his paper back, it looked terrible. At the top, Mrs. Wix had written, "Great story." But she drew bloody red circles around all the misspelled words. Lots of them!

Montgomery was supposed to correct all the misspellings and turn the story back in. But he didn't do it. He'd started to. But he got so tired trying to look up all those words in the dictionary. He couldn't even find half of them. His mom would've helped. But he didn't want to show her the paper with all the measles.

Next time, Montgomery decided, he'd write a very short story. Maybe he'd write about those male flying ants that die a couple hours after they're born. They don't ever eat or anything. His story would say: "Once a flying male ant was born. Then he died. The end—of the ant and the story."

# Ten

**G**et out a fresh sheet of paper," said Mrs. Wix. "Number your papers from one to twenty. I'll say each spelling word twice and use it in a sentence. You just write the word. Ready? Number one. *Elephant. Elephant.* An *elephant* is a large jungle animal."

Montgomery's hands were sweaty. He

wiped them on his pants. They were sweaty again by the time they reached his paper.

He glanced at Beatrice. She was writing away, looking cool as ice. When she finished writing, Beatrice cupped her hand over her paper. She wanted to protect her answers from spelling robbers.

Montgomery wiped his hand again and started to spell. He remembered that *elephant* had a silly *p* in the middle. E-L-I-P-U-N-T, he wrote.

Mrs. Wix paced as she dictated the rest of the words. The charms on her bracelet yapped like angry little puppies. "Yap! Yap!" they scolded Montgomery. "You don't know your spelling words!"

One hour later, Mrs. Wix walked up and down the rows and handed back the spelling tests. The good ones, that is. Montgomery hoped beyond hope. Maybe he had done okay. Sometimes you know more than you think you know, he told himself. He had sounded out every word. Just maybe . . .

Mrs. Wix gave Beatrice back her paper.

Montgomery peeked over. Beatrice's hand wasn't hiding her paper now. A big **110%** was written across the top. Mrs. Wix had made a smiley face in the zero.

Mrs. Wix was walking toward Montgomery now. Montgomery could sense her reaching into the stack for his paper. He could almost feel her about to put it on his desk.

But she walked on by. Nothing was left behind but the slight breeze of her passing.

When Mrs. Wix finished handing out the tests, she went to the front of the room. She still had three papers left.

A hush fell over the class. It was as if someone had just said, "Shhh, time for court."

# Eleven

**M**rs. Wix called Ju-Ju Bee to the front of the class first. "Julius," she said. Her voice rumbled.

Ju-Ju Bee tapped on desks as he walked up to the front. Mrs. Wix frowned. Ju-Ju Bee didn't seem to notice. The teacher opened her mouth to say something, but Ju-Ju Bee just reached up and took his paper. By the time he turned around, he had rolled his paper into a drumstick to tap on the desks on his way back. As soon as Ju-Ju Bee got back to his seat, he stuffed the spelling paper inside his desk.

Kathy was next. She was a very quiet girl. Twice before she had been called to the front after spelling tests. Kathy had a ponytail. It bobbed as she walked up to Mrs. Wix.

Montgomery watched as Kathy kept nodding her head. It looked like she was saying yes, even though Mrs. Wix hadn't said anything yet.

Mrs. Wix handed Kathy her paper. Then Mrs. Wix leaned forward and said something to her. Kathy didn't say anything, but her ponytail wagged and wagged.

Mrs. Wix had one paper left. The class waited quietly. She looked down at the name on the paper. "Montgomery Thornton," she said.

Montgomery weaved up the aisle. He bumped into a desk. For some reason, he couldn't seem to walk straight.

When he got to the front, Montgomery reached for his paper. But Mrs. Wix held on to it. Montgomery knew everybody was watching. The class was so quiet. He could feel all their ears bent toward him, like a cat's toward a sound. Montgomery could *feel* all those pairs of eyes glued on him.

"Spelling isn't your best subject, is it, Montgomery?" said Mrs. Wix. She spoke so quietly that not even cat's ears could hear.

"I guess not," Montgomery answered. His face felt hot. He knew it was purple—as purple as the gum that couldn't be hidden in Ju-Ju Bee's ear.

"I think we can change that. Would you like to try?"

"I guess so."

It was strange. Mrs. Wix was frowning. But she didn't seem angry. Just concerned.

Mrs. Wix turned to her desk. She opened the drawer and pulled something out. The little instrument she handed him looked something like a calculator. "It's called a Spell Check," said Mrs. Wix. "You type in the word and it tells you how to spell it." Mrs. Wix was still whispering. "Can you come in early on Monday, Montgomery? You and I could work with it together."

"Okay."

"Good. By the way, where's that wonderful story about the whale? You have a gift for storytelling, Montgomery." Mrs. Wix wasn't whispering anymore. "I think that story would be a good one to tape-record for the class. Do you think you could prepare some sound effects?"

"I guess so." Guess so? Montgomery *knew* so. Loud whale snorts? He and Ben could handle that, no problem.

Mrs. Wix held on to the paper one more second before handing it over. Long enough to do something amazing. Her frown turned upside down.

Mrs. Wix smiled at Montgomery.

# Twelve

**M**ontgomery walked back to his seat. The class was already busy getting ready for math. Sounds of activity filled the classroom. Desktops were lifted, papers shuffled, books opened.

Montgomery sat down. As he got out his

math stuff, his pencil dropped. Beatrice quickly leaned over and picked it up. She started to hand it back, then noticed the dull point. "Just a minute," she whispered.

Beatrice reached for the sharpener she kept in her desk. She put the pencil inside and gave several quick flicks. Then she examined the point, gave a *wiff!* to blow away the scraps, and handed it back to Montgomery with a proud smile.

"Thanks," he said.

The heat was gone from Montgomery's cheeks.

It was over.

It was really over.

Mrs. Wix was already asking a question about math. Beatrice already had her hand up.

Soon the class was buzzing about fractions. Mrs. Wix was demonstrating how to do a problem on the chalkboard.

Montgomery sat there feeling . . . Suddenly he realized he was feeling terrific!

The worst had happened.

He had flunked.

He had made the march (or the stumble) to the front of the room.

Yet here he was. Here they all were. Montgomery looked around. Ben had on his thinking frown. Ju-Ju Bee was scratching his ear. Beatrice scribbled notes. He felt he liked his class so much. Everybody!

And Mrs. Wix was going to help him with spelling. Maybe that Spell Check *could* help. Who knew?

Mrs. Wix was tapping one of the numbers

on the board with a piece of chalk. The charms on her bracelet moved. They jingled and danced with a merry tune.

After school, the bus was late. The driver called in to say he had a flat tire. There was just enough time for a quick game of baseball.

"We get Montgomery!"

"No, we do!"

Montgomery was cleanup hitter. One guy was on base when he stepped up to the plate.

A frisky wind blew through Montgomery's hair. The wind also seemed to blow right through him, filling him with fresh air. Big tall trees around the playground were waving in the breeze, bending and swaying. They looked ready to play, as well.

The first pitch came. High and outside. Ball one.

Montgomery stepped away from the plate and took a practice swing. The bat felt so natural in his hands. He loved the narrow grip, the heavier weight at the end. It felt like the bat was a part of him. Montgomery loved swinging it, too, putting his whole body into it.

Another pitch. Low and outside.

Third pitch. Montgomery saw it coming, as if in slow motion. He let go with everything he had. *Whop!*

Montgomery didn't even have to look at the ball. He could feel what he'd done down to his very bones. All his power had somehow rushed to the end of his bat. He knew that the ball was sailing out into space. But he took a look anyway.

And it was. That ball was soaring, up, up to meet a sea-blue sky. It looked as if the ball was aiming to make a hole through a white cloud. And that ball just might do it, too.